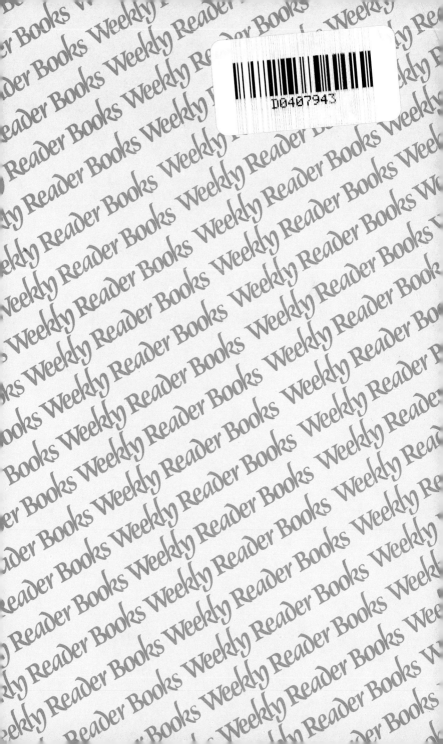

THE MYSTERY OF THE DINOSAUR BONES

BOOKS BY MARY ADRIAN

THE AMERICAN MUSTANG
THE AMERICAN EAGLE
THE SKIN DIVING MYSTERY
THE MYSTERY OF THE NIGHT EXPLORERS
THE RARE STAMP MYSTERY
THE FOX HOLLOW MYSTERY
JONATHAN CROW, DETECTIVE
THE URANIUM MYSTERY
REFUGEE HERO
Hastings House

GARDEN SPIDER
HONEYBEE
FIDDLER CRAB
GRAY SQUIRREL
Holiday House

THE FIREHOUSE MYSTERY
THE TUGBOAT MYSTERY
Houghton Mifflin Co.

THE HIDDEN SPRING MYSTERY
THE JUNIOR SHERIFF MYSTERY
Ariel Books,
Farrar, Straus & Co.

Weekly Reader Books presents

The
Mystery of
THE
DINOSAUR
BONES

by MARY ADRIAN

Text Illustrated by Lloyd Coe

HASTINGS HOUSE • PUBLISHERS

New York

COPYRIGHT © 1965 by Mary Adrian

All rights reserved. No part of
this book may be reproduced
without written permission
of the publisher.

Published simultaneously in Canada
by Saunders of Toronto, Ltd.
Don Mills, Ontario
ISBN: 8038–4644–4

Library of Congress Catalog Card Number: 64–8119

Printed in the United States of America

Contents

CHAPTER ONE

The Secret Letter

Chris and Ken were twins. They had blue eyes, freckles, and bright red hair. Chris liked her hair, especially when friends told her how pretty it was. Her brother felt differently because boys often called him "Red." This made him furious, and he would explain loftily that his name was Kenneth—Ken for short.

Chris never bothered to tell anyone that her real name was Christine. She enjoyed being called Chris.

This Friday morning she and her brother were cleaning the house. A warm summer breeze came in through the living-room windows. Chris was on her knees dusting the legs of the coffee table. Ken was running the vacuum cleaner over the rug.

"We're wasting our time," Ken shouted above the noise of the vacuum cleaner. "We should be packing and not cleaning a house that will be closed for two weeks. Dad won't like it if our camping things aren't in the car when he comes home tonight. He said we're leaving early tomorrow morning for the Pacific Coast."

"Mother says the house should not be left dirty when we start out on Dad's vacation," Chris called back.

Ken scowled and grumbled to himself. After he had finished cleaning the rug, he took the plug out of the electric outlet and headed for his room down the hall, pulling the vacuum after him. He gave his rug a complete going over, but avoided cleaning under his bed, for he felt no one ever looked there. Besides, he had a number of snakeskins under the bed. In the spring Ken had combed the neighboring fields for the cast-off skins. His aim was to collect fifty of them, and he had found twenty, but his sister had a horror of snakes, so he kept the skins in hiding.

Ken turned off the vacuum and was about to

count his snakeskins for the nth time when a familiar squeaking brake made him rush to the front screen door. The postman was leaning out of his truck, stuffing all sorts of things into their mailbox.

"Yippee! The mailman is here!" Ken shouted, dashing out of the house.

Chris followed, a second behind her brother. For a week she and Ken had been looking for a letter from Marty Taylor. He lived down their street, on the outskirts of Salt Lake City, and was eleven years old—the same age as Chris and Ken. Marty had gone on a camping trip with his parents to dinosaur country in Utah, and had promised to write to his friends.

The three children had read books on dinosaurs, and their one desire was to go dinosaur hunting. They knew that dinosaurs lived millions of years ago, and that they were strange-looking reptiles. They also knew that dinosaur bones had been found in rocks, and that they had become fossilized, that is, turned to stone.

Now that Marty was camping in dinosaur country, he was the envy of Chris and Ken, and they were waiting anxiously to hear from him. So this morning the twins asked the mailman three times if there was a letter from Marty. Before he could answer, Ken took it for granted that there was not.

"Shucks," he said. "I guess Marty isn't having any luck at dinosaur hunting."

"There *is* a letter for us," squealed Chris, catching the mailman's mischievous expression.

"You win," he answered. "I put it in the box first—just to keep you in suspense."

Eager hands reached into the box and pulled out a small package, bills, a sample cake of soap, a magazine, and last, the important letter with Marty's name on the back of the envelope. It was addressed to Ken Rockhill.

Chris pursed her lips in disappointment. "I wish Marty had put my name on the envelope too. Hurry. Open it, Ken," she added, jumping up and down with excitement.

Ken took the envelope and began tearing the flap in a zigzag fashion.

Chris was sure he was tearing the letter into pieces. "Let me do it," she begged.

Ken reluctantly handed her the envelope. In a jiffy Chris pulled out the letter. It was a blank piece of white paper.

The mailman roared with laughter, his plump

sides shaking like jelly. "Your friend sure is playing a trick on you."

"Oh, no, he isn't," replied Chris seriously. "Marty has written a secret letter on this piece of paper. He only does that when he has something very important to tell us."

Leaving the mailman staring after them in wonderment, the twins raced back to the house. The screen door banged behind them. They gulped at their mother's disapproving look.

"I'm sorry I slammed the door," muttered Chris.

"Me too," echoed Ken, rushing over to a lamp in the living room.

"Where is the mail?" asked Mrs. Rockhill.

"Ken, we left it by the mailbox," wailed Chris. "I'll get it. Don't do anything until I come back."

"I won't," he replied. Ken kept turning over the blank piece of paper and tapping his foot impatiently.

"What's the matter with you, Ken?" asked his mother. "You're acting like a fly batting against a windowpane. And what's that piece of paper in your hand?"

Fortunately Ken did not have to answer. Chris came in with the rest of the mail, and Mrs. Rockhill was so glad to see the package that she began removing the wrappings right away. Mrs. Rockhill was a birdwatcher and had ordered a book on the subject.

Ken took off the lamp shade and turned on the light. Holding the blank piece of paper over the electric bulb, he and Chris watched the writing come into view. Then they started reading Marty's secret letter.

> Dear Ken and Chris:
>
> My parents will phone Friday night and try and get your dad to change his mind and come here for his vacation. You do your part before the phone rings.
>
> I went dinosaur hunting with a swell person called Winkie. A friend left him a map that shows where there is a dinosaur graveyard, but Winkie can't find it even with the map. Since his friend is dead, Winkie says more eyes would help in searching for the graveyard. So here's hoping you can come. Be sure and bring your dinosaur-hunting equipment along.
>
> Your friend,
Marty
>
> P.S. There are plenty of spooky sounds here at night. Big animals must be prowling around.

"Golly," breathed Chris. "What a letter!" She read it a second time.

Ken read it a third time, but all he kept saying

was "Wow," until Mrs. Rockhill became curious. "Why are you holding that piece of paper over a lighted electric bulb?" she asked him.

"So we can read a secret message, Mom," explained Ken.

"A secret message on a blank piece of paper?" Mrs. Rockhill was interested.

"Yes," answered Chris. "You see, Marty used lemon juice instead of ink when he wrote this letter. The only way you can read it is over a lighted electric bulb. That's what makes it a secret letter."

Mrs. Rockhill smiled. "What will you children think of doing next? Is Marty having fun?"

"I'll say he is," replied Ken. "He went dinosaur hunting. Just think of that, Mom. Dinosaur hunting! Boy, that's the life." Then Ken added in a serious voice, "Er . . . Mr. and Mrs. Taylor are going to phone tonight. They want us to come there."

Mrs. Rockhill frowned. "Don't they know that Dad has already made plans for his vacation?" she asked.

"Oh, yes," answered Chris. "We told Marty we were driving to the Pacific Coast because Dad likes to go deep-sea fishing there. Couldn't we go to both places?" Chris pleaded with her big blue eyes. "Please, Mother?"

Mrs. Rockhill sadly shook her head. "I'm afraid it's hard to change Dad when he makes up his mind to do something."

"I know," sighed Chris, "but not many children get the chance to go dinosaur hunting. Marty wants us to help look for a dinosaur graveyard, and it would make Grandma happy if we used the dinosaur tools she gave Ken and me at Christmas. This way they just sit in the closet."

"That's right," agreed Ken. "What good are the tools if you don't work with them?"

"We'll see," said Mrs. Rockhill as she turned back to reading her bird book. The twins decided she did not wish to talk any more about Dad's vacation.

That evening at dinner, however, Ken and Chris tried very hard to persuade their father to go to Marty's camp.

"It's out of the question," he replied. "Maybe next year you can look for dinosaur bones."

Chris stopped eating and folded her hands in her lap. The food on her plate no longer tasted good.

Ken felt the same way, but he and his sister

perked up when the phone rang a few moments later and Mrs. Rockhill spoke to Mrs. Taylor.

"How wonderful to hear your voice, Laura," she said. "That bird book you recommended came in the mail today. It's going to be very helpful." There was a pause and then Mrs. Rockhill continued, "You say there are many different kinds of birds where you are. My, I'd give anything to see them."

Chris looked at Ken and grinned. Mother seemed very interested and that was a good sign.

However, when Dad took the receiver and talked to Marty's father, things did not appear very promising. "No, Sam," he said, "we're all set to drive to the Pacific Coast. We leave tomorrow morning at dawn. I'm sorry, but my heart is set on deep-sea fishing."

The twins hung their heads in disappointment. Suddenly they heard their father say, "There is good fishing where you are? Hm. Sounds tempting, Sam. Yes, very tempting."

Ken took a deep breath, and Chris crossed her fingers, hoping Dad would change his mind. He finally did, for the telephone conversation ended as he replied, "Okay, Sam. We'll see you tomorrow. Save us a camp site."

The twins hugged each other with joy.

"Just think of it, Ken!" exclaimed Chris. "We're going dinosaur hunting."

Her brother nodded, his cheeks flushed with excitement. "Boy, I can hardly wait to get to Marty's camp."

"Me too." Then Chris shivered. She was thinking about the spooky noises Marty had mentioned in his secret letter. But she must not act like a scaredy cat, she told herself. After all, this was going to be a big adventure.

CHAPTER TWO

The Map

The Rockhill family left for Marty's camp Saturday afternoon. Their station wagon rolled along the highway, with Dad at the wheel and Mother in the front seat next to him. The twins were sitting in the back, looking at their dinosaur tools—a small pick, chisel, shovel, and rock hammer.

"I wish I was going dinosaur hunting right now," said Ken.

"So do I," added Chris. "How far is it to Marty's camp, Daddy?"

"Two hundred and fifty miles," replied Mr. Rockhill.

18

"How long do you think it will take us to get there?" asked Ken.

"Oh, we should make it in two days." Mr. Rockhill tried to keep from smiling.

"Two days!" roared Ken. "Why a snail could travel faster than that."

Mr. Rockhill laughed. "We're averaging fifty miles an hour, Ken. So you tell me how long it will take us to get there."

"It will . . . er . . . "

"Five hours if we don't stop on the way," finished Chris.

"Yes, five hours," repeated Ken. Then, turning to his sister, he said in anger, "You didn't have to tell me. I knew it all the time."

"Of course you did," said Mrs. Rockhill.

Ken grinned. He felt better.

In a little while he and his sister were getting restless.

"Could you please stop somewhere, Daddy? My seat aches," said Chris.

"We will at the next rest area."

Mr. Rockhill soon drove into a shady place near a stream, and everyone got out of the station wagon. The twins headed for the drinking fountain. They were still taking turns drinking when their parents returned to the station wagon a short while later.

"We'd better go, Ken," said Chris.

"Okay," he answered.

As soon as Ken and his sister had scrambled into their places the Rockhill family continued their journey. At seven o'clock that evening they were still driving.

Chris yawned and then said in a mournful voice, "All we do is ride, ride, ride. Of course we did stop at three rest areas on the way, but I guess by this time Marty must think we're not coming."

"In another fifteen minutes we should be seeing the Taylors," said Mr. Rockhill.

"Honest, Daddy? You're not spoofing?" asked Chris.

"No, I really mean it."

Ken's eyes sparkled with excitement. He stuck two fingers in his mouth and whistled. It was a shrill whistle that made Chris put her hands over her ears, but she laughed just the same.

A short while later Chris sat up straight in her seat and shouted, "There's Marty. Hi, Marty! Hi, Marty!"

Marty was sitting on the top of a big boulder at

the entrance to the camp grounds. On seeing the Rockhills, he jumped down from his perch with the swiftness of a squirrel and waved his arms.

Mr. Rockhill stopped the car, and Marty climbed into the back seat.

"I'm sure glad you could come," he said, giving Ken a playful punch in the ribs. He slapped Chris on the back in a friendly way and pulled her hair.

"Ouch!" she squealed and then giggled. She could not be cross with Marty. That was his way of saying "Hi."

Marty also told Mr. and Mrs. Rockhill how happy he was to see them. "You drive down this road until you come to camp site ten," he said to Mr. Rockhill. "That's where we are. We saved camp site twelve for you. A couple checked out of there this morning." Marty turned to the twins. "Winkie is at camp site fourteen next to you. Tomorrow we're going to look for the dinosaur graveyard, and he wants you to come along."

"Golly! That's wonderful!" Chris pinched herself to make sure she wasn't dreaming.

Ken was as thrilled as his sister. "Now we can use our dinosaur tools, Chris. I'll bet we'll be the best dinosaur hunters in the country."

"I don't doubt it," said Mr. Rockhill, with a laugh. "Did your dad catch any fish today, Marty?"

"Yes. Ten big trout. We're going to have them for supper. Mom said that the Rockhill family is to eat with us."

"Ten trout!" repeated Mr. Rockhill, grinning like a Cheshire cat.

"Mom is planning to show you all kinds of birds, Mrs. Rockhill," continued Marty. "I saw some the other day. They sure were pretty."

Mrs. Rockhill purred like a kitten.

The station wagon stopped in front of the Taylors' camp site where an umbrella tent stood in a fairly large area. Mrs. Taylor was taking down wash from a clothesline hanging between two trees. She quickly put the wash on the picnic table and hurried to meet the Rockhills. So did Mr. Taylor, who was fixing his fishing tackle in front of the tent. Then he and Mrs. Taylor told the Rockhills how glad they were to see them.

After dinner, while the men talked about fishing, and the women about birds, the children set out to look for Winkie. They went to his camp site, but he was not there.

"We'll go to the Bronsons' trailer," said Marty.

"Winkie likes to hang out there."

He led the way down a short bank to another road, where a large white trailer was nestled under some trees. Mr. Bronson was reading in a comfortable chair outside. His black cocker spaniel was sitting at his feet, scratching flea bites.

Marty coughed to let Mr. Bronson know he was there, and then said in a polite voice, "I'm sorry to disturb you, Mr. Bronson, but have you seen Winkie?"

"Nope," answered the man, looking up over his glasses. "He's late making the rounds this evening. I don't know where he's keeping himself."

Marty snapped his fingers. "I'll bet he's meditating on his log near the river."

"Meditating?" Chris was puzzled.

"That's what Winkie calls it when he's thinking about the dinosaur graveyard," explained Marty. "He studies his map and meditates. Come on. I'll race you down to the river. The last one there is a dead fish."

With the speed of a rocket, Marty tore through some brush near the road. The twins ran after him. They jumped over a big log and several rocks. They dashed on, with Marty still in the lead. Ken came next, and then Chris, but suddenly she sprinted forward and passed her brother.

A few moments later the race ended, with Marty coming in first, Chris second, and Ken last.

"You're a dead fish, Ken," cried Chris gleefully. It was the first time she had outrun her brother.

Ken grumbled and then forgot about being angry with himself, for Marty was introducing him to Winkie, a thin, wiry old man with white hair. He was sitting on a log studying his map as Marty had predicted.

"Howdee, Chris and Ken," he said in a jovial voice. "Marty has told me all about you, and I'm glad you could come. We're having a time finding the dinosaur graveyard. This map has us baffled." He spread out a piece of paper on the log for them to examine.

The twins got down on their knees and looked curiously at the crude map that Winkie's friend had drawn. They could see the drawings of some trees and a big boulder. There were also two cliffs. One was shaped like the hump on a camel's back. The other cliff had a big hole in the side of the wall. On the bottom of the map was written in large letters: TO FIND LOCATION OF DINOSAUR GRAVEYARD. The next word was blurred. After it came: CAMEL-BACK CLIFF. Then another word was blurred. It was followed by: HOLE IN THE WALL.

Chris frowned. "Golly, it's hard to understand what those words are on the map. Does it mean that there are two clues—the camel-back cliff and the cliff with a big hole?"

"Yes," answered Winkie, "but Marty and I haven't found cliffs that look like either of those."

Ken was still studying the map. "Maybe when we do find them, we'll know what the blurred words mean."

"That's what Winkie and I think," said Marty. "It isn't easy, though, to spot those two cliffs."

"It's like searching for a needle in a haystack," added Winkie, "with all the cliffs around here. There must be fifty or more."

"Then it will be like going on a treasure hunt," said Chris. "You keep looking until you find the treasure."

Winkie smiled. "That's exactly what you do. Dinosaur hunting takes a lot of patience. You just don't find dinosaur bones like shells on a beach, but when you do discover one, it *is* like finding a treasure. I'll never forget how thrilled I was when I found part of a dinosaur's rib on the side of a cliff in Wyoming. In this country I haven't had any luck, although some dinosaur hunters have. That's why I was so happy to get my friend's map. I was sure it would help me find a dinosaur graveyard, but I didn't realize it would be so hard to locate a camel-back cliff and one with a big hole."

"We'll track down the two clues," said Ken.

"We certainly will," added Chris. "When Mother loses something, Ken and I always find it for her. Daddy says that's because we have sharp eyes. So I'm positive we'll find the dinosaur graveyard."

"Boy, you've got me excited," said Marty. "I'm surely going to look for those two cliffs when we go dinosaur hunting tomorrow. I wonder which one of us will spot them first?"

"I hope it's me," said Chris.

"I'll bet I beat you to it," said Ken.

Winkie laughed. He was moved by the children's enthusiasm. "You've convinced me that we will come across that graveyard." He paused and then said, "I guess you already see that it is fascinating to look for the remains of those big reptiles and put the different parts of their skeletons together. Just think of it! Dinosaurs were roaming on this earth two hundred million years ago!"

"There were still some dinosaurs living sixty million years ago," added Marty. "Then they died out, and that was the end of the Age of Reptiles. I learned that from a book."

"But no one really knows why the dinosaurs died," chimed in Chris.

Ken also wanted to furnish some information. "Some scientists think that there wasn't enough food for all the dinosaurs. Others wonder if it was because the climate changed. It was hot, as it is in the tropics, when the dinosaurs lived. Anyway, it sure is a mystery what happened to them."

"My, you children do know something about dinosaurs," said Winkie. "I'm glad, because that really makes you want to hunt for the graveyard, and I'm counting on you to find it."

Marty and the twins grinned with pride. They were so happy that Winkie wanted their help that the boys did several handsprings and Chris hopped with delight from one foot to the other. Then she looked at the map and studied the drawings of the cliffs.

Later, after she had gone to bed, the map came to her thoughts again.

"Ken," she said, "what do you think the two smudged words are on Winkie's map?"

Her brother did not answer. He was dead to the world, curled up in his sleeping bag.

Mother and Dad were also asleep, but Chris could not keep her eyes closed. Suddenly she was sitting bolt upright, listening to a weird sound.

CHAPTER THREE

The Shadow

The shrill noise that Chris had just heard was the distant cry of a coyote. She had forgotten about the spooky sounds mentioned in Marty's secret letter, because Winkie's map had been on her mind.

Now, as Chris listened to the coyote screaming, she trembled from head to toe.

"Ken," she whispered. "Wake up. Wake up."

Her brother did not stir. He continued to breathe heavily, and Chris, scowling, lay back in her sleeping bag. She hoped the terrible screams would stop. They soon did, but to her dismay she heard other sounds. First came the eerie call of an owl. Then the wind began to blow, and the leaves of the cottonwood trees near the tent rustled like tissue paper.

Chris wished they had not camped under the trees. It would have been safer if they had pitched their tent in the open. This way an animal could easily drop from a tree onto the top of the tent. What kind of an animal, she asked herself? Well, it could be a bear. Chris swallowed hard as she thought about it.

Presently the wind died down to a low murmur. Chris was about to doze off when a scratching sound outside made her as rigid as a rabbit sensing danger.

Again she tried to wake Ken, but he did not budge. So Chris listened to the scratching noise until it finally stopped. She was glad then that she had not awakened her brother. He would certainly have called her a scaredy cat; and she must be brave during her stay at camp, even though she didn't like all these spooky sounds.

A few moments later she heard a noise close to the tent that sounded like a person prowling around. This was too much for Chris. She reached over and gave Ken such a sharp poke in the ribs that he awoke with a start.

"Ken," she whispered. "There's someone outside. It might be a burglar."

"Man! We'd better see," he whispered back.

Soon Chris and her brother were peering out the screen door of the tent. Moonlight filtered through the cottonwood trees, making the ground look like silver. The twins could see no one around, and the only noise that broke the stillness was somebody snoring in the tent to the left of them.

"You're imagining things," said Ken. "Let's go back to bed."

"No, I'm not," protested Chris. "I just saw a shadow move under that tree over there."

Together she and Ken stared at the shadow. They saw it grow longer and longer in the moonlight. Suddenly a tall, thin, bald-headed man came into view. He was wearing dark pants and a jacket.

The twins watched the man walk toward the road and disappear among some trees.

"I'm sure he's a burglar," said Chris. "Did you see how he held his hand on his hip? I'll bet he's got a gun in his pocket."

"I wouldn't be surprised," answered Ken. He was about to say more when a voice said, "What are you children doing?" Their mother was sitting up in bed looking at them.

"Er . . . we just saw someone outside," explained Chris. "I'm sure he's a burglar."

Mrs. Rockhill laughed. "There are no burglars around here. It was probably a camper heading for the rest room. Now go back to sleep."

The talking awakened Mr. Rockhill. "Anything wrong?" he asked in a sleepy voice.

"Oh, the children heard someone outside. They thought it was a burglar, but I told them it was only another camper."

"Sure. That's who it was." Mr. Rockhill rolled over on his side and chuckled. "You'd better not tell your friend Marty about this. He'd never stop teasing you."

The twins did not answer. They crawled back into their sleeping bags, wondering if the man had stolen something from the camp. Chris wanted to talk to her brother about it, but she realized she must wait until morning. She closed her eyes and tried very hard to go to sleep.

It was not long before she was wide awake again. So were her parents and Ken—all listening to loud screams nearby.

"Heavens!" exclaimed Mrs. Rockhill in alarm.

"It sounds as if somebody is being murdered."

A few moments later all four Rockhills were standing outside the tent in their bathrobes.

Winkie and Mrs. Winkle joined them shortly.

"What on earth is going on?" he asked, running his fingers through his rumpled hair.

"You've got me," replied Mr. Rockhill. "I wish I knew."

Just then Marty rushed up to the twins and said, "Boy, this is exciting. I wonder what's going to happen next?"

"I do too," said Chris.

She and the boys listened to the cries, which now sounded louder.

Soon voices came from other tents and trailers, and before long the camp ground was filled with curious people standing about in their night clothes.

The twins were convinced that the man they had seen a little while ago had robbed a camper. They were all set to tell Marty about him when a person yelled out, "Aw, it's only someone having a bad dream."

After that another person shouted, "There's nothing to be disturbed about, folks. A man just awoke from an awful nightmare."

The children looked disappointed. Then Chris and her brother followed their parents into the tent, and Marty headed for his camp site.

After that all was quiet in the camp grounds. People went back to sleep. Chris lay awake a little while but dozed off presently. When she awoke the next morning, she heard Marty say outside the tent, "Ken, you'd better wake up Chris. Winkie doesn't like to be kept waiting when he's going dinosaur hunting."

"I'll be there in a jiffy," Chris called to the boys.

She slipped into her clothes and, after grabbing a knapsack with dinosaur tools sticking out of it, went outside.

Ken was having breakfast at the camp table. Marty had eaten an early breakfast and was enjoying a second one.

Chris sat down at the table. She wanted to eat quickly, but under her mother's watchful eye, she took small bites.

As soon as breakfast was over, the twins and Marty washed and dried the dishes. Mrs. Rockhill prepared a picnic lunch for them and put a paper bag with sandwiches and fruit in each of their packs.

After that the children hurried to Winkie's camp site, carrying their knapsacks. There they found the old man and Mrs. Winkle on their knees, peering under the table.

"Are you looking for something?" asked Marty.

"Yes," answered Winkie, getting to his feet and sitting down on a chair. "I left the map in my fossil book on this table last night. This morning I found the book wide open and no map in it."

"Are you sure you put the map in your fossil book, dear?" asked Mrs. Winkle. She was still searching under the table. "Often I think I've laid something in a certain place, and when I look for it, I find it in another place."

Winkie thought a moment. "No. I'm positive the map was in my fossil book."

"We'll start hunting for it right away," said Marty.

As the twins began looking around the tent, Marty went to the refuse can close by. He felt that since his mother had once put a valuable fork in the trash can by mistake, Winkie might have done the same with the map. Besides, he wanted to see if a camper had thrown away any newspapers. Marty's hobby was reading, and his room at home was stacked with books, magazines, and other material that he had collected.

Right now Marty grinned with delight as he pulled a newspaper out of the trash can. On the front page was the picture of a dark-haired man with bushy eyebrows. On the same page were pictures of two boys who had discovered the fossilized bones of a prehistoric camel in Oregon. Marty wanted to read about the boys' find, but feeling it would take too long, he laid the newspaper down and continued rummaging through the trash can. After seeing no trace of Winkie's map, he picked up the paper, dashed to his tent, and stuffed it in his sleeping bag for future use. Then he ran back to Winkie's camp site.

"Have you found the map?" he asked him.

"No," answered Winkie. "I only hope someone didn't go off with it."

Chris and Ken looked at each other wide-eyed. All they could think of was that the bald-headed man they had seen during the night had taken the map. They quickly told Winkie and Marty about him.

"He was a stranger, all right," said Marty, "because there is no bald-headed man in this camp. I'll bet he stole the map."

"That is something we don't know for sure,"

said Winkie. "The man might have been driving by and stopped to go to the rest room. On the other hand, it *is* mysterious the way my map disappeared." He gave a big sigh. "Well, I guess if we're going to hunt for the dinosaur graveyard, we'd better leave soon."

"We're ready right now," replied three eager children.

CHAPTER FOUR

The Dinosaur Hunt

After the twins and Marty put their knapsacks in the rear of Winkie's red pick-up truck, they climbed in the front seat. A few moments later Winkie started the truck, and it began moving toward the exit of the camp grounds. Some campers waved good-by. The children waved back and then laughed at a dog who was racing after the truck.

"Man! Can that dog run!" exclaimed Marty.

"He sure can," agreed Ken.

The dog was still dashing after the truck when Winkie steered onto the highway, but soon after that he gave up the chase. Panting, he turned and headed toward the camp ground.

The truck jogged along for quite a distance before Winkie turned onto a narrow road that zigzagged through a river valley. This road was so bumpy that the children bounced and swayed; but they were enjoying every minute of the ride, and they liked looking at the passing countryside.

Chris saw a jackrabbit jump toward some brush to dodge the truck. She pointed out the rabbit to the boys.

Then Ken spotted a black and white animal near the side of the road.

"Hey, there's a skunk," he shouted.

"That's the first time I've seen one in the daytime," remarked Marty. "A skunk is a night prowler."

"Yes, it is," agreed Winkie, "but occasionally a skunk will come out during the day."

Winkie then steered onto another rough road. Flat-topped mountains showed in the distance. Closer up were cliffs, their purple and red sides gleaming in the sunlight.

The children gazed at the different cliffs with their ragged tops, but they could not see one shaped like a camel's back. Neither was there a cliff with a big hole.

"Shucks," groaned Ken. "I guess it's not going to be easy to find the two clues."

Marty looked at his friend in surprise. "Don't tell me you've given up hunting for them already?"

"Of course not," snapped Ken. "What do you take me for?"

Finally Winkie stopped the truck. "All out, passengers," he said. "We've come to the end of the line. Now it's time to use your legs. Take your dinosaur equipment with you."

The children lost no time getting their knapsacks from the back of the truck. Soon they were hiking with Winkie through a canyon—a deep valley with high, sloping cliffs. Some were bare. Others were covered with brush and a few trees.

As Winkie focused his binoculars on the cliffs in the distance, the children gathered around him.

"Do you see a clue?" asked Marty.

"No," replied Winkie, sadly shaking his head. "I guess we're on the wrong track, but let's find out what the land is like at the end of this canyon."

"May I please use your binoculars?" Marty asked eagerly.

"Sure," said Winkie, handing him the field glasses. "You might spot something that I missed."

After Marty had studied the different cliffs, he gave the binoculars to Ken, who in turn passed them on to Chris. She was so fascinated with the glasses that she kept on looking until Ken called, "Chris, don't stay there all night."

She hurried to catch up with the others who were walking along a rocky river bed. Then Chris stopped to gather some brightly colored stones; but she took so long that soon she was again behind the others, and her brother had to call her a second time.

Chris ran along the river bed as best she could.

"I'm sorry," she said when she reached Winkie and the boys waiting for her at the end of the canyon.

"We'll accept your apology," said Ken, "but for Pete's sake stay with us from now on," he added sharply.

Chris gulped. "I will," she promised in a small voice and then looked at a stretch of desert before her. On one side was a hogback mountain. On the other side were cliffs with sloping terraces.

Chris shaded her eyes with her hands to get a better view of the cliffs in the sunlight. The boys squinted and moved to one side, hoping to see them better, but the sun still shone in their faces. So the children were happy when Winkie suggested walking to the cliffs.

Slowly they started hiking across the desert. They went by sagebrush that appeared as dry as the parched earth that held its roots. They passed a lot of greasewood—shrubs with sharp, prickly leaves. And they wound their way around some cactus. All the while the sun was getting hotter and hotter, but the children did not complain. They were glad, though, when Winkie finally decided to stop and rest under a tree.

It was then that Chris saw a large opening near the bottom of one of the cliffs.

"I found a clue," she shouted. "There's a hole in the side of that cliff over there. See it."

The boys and Winkie stared at the deep gash.

"It's not the kind of hole that was drawn on the map, Chris," said Marty.

"No, it isn't," added Ken.

Chris's face clouded with disappointment. "Oh, dear. I thought I'd spotted a clue."

Winkie patted her on the shoulder. "Never mind. We'll investigate that deep gash, anyway."

Chris looked at him with a grateful smile, and soon they were all walking to the cliff, which was a quarter of a mile away. Chris and the boys wanted to run, but did not feel it was right to do so until they came within a few yards of it. Then all three of them broke loose at once. With arms and legs flying they raced to the opening in the side of the cliff. There they found a scattering of rocks, their pink, yellow, and white colors blending like those in a rainbow.

Winkie arrived a few moments later. He immediately examined the large gash. "Why, this is a dinosaur quarry!" he exclaimed. "I've heard that a paleontologist discovered a whole skeleton in this country. This must be the place where he dug out the bones."

"Pay-lee-on-tol-o-gist," repeated Chris slowly, so that she would not forget how to pronounce it. "Is that the name of a person who studies dinosaur bones?"

Winkie nodded. "Maybe someday you'll be a paleontologist."

"I hope so." Chris was thinking how wonderful it would be to have a long name like that.

"What kind of dinosaur skeleton did the paleontologist find?" asked Marty, glad to show that he could pronounce it, too.

"An Allosaurus," answered Winkie.

"How big was it?" Ken asked.

"It was thirty-five feet long," replied the old man. "The skeleton is mounted in a museum in a large city."

"I saw the skeleton of Brontosaurus in a museum, Winkie," said Marty. "That's the thunder lizard. It was seventy feet long and weighed thirty-five tons."

Winkie did not look surprised. "I don't doubt it. Brontosaurus was one of the larger dinosaurs. Because it weighed so much it liked to stand in swamps where the water helped to hold it up. I guess it ate plants all day long. Now Allosaurus was a meat-eater. It ate other dinosaurs as big as Brontosaurus. We know this to be true because a Brontosaurus skeleton was found in Wyoming with the tooth marks of Allosaurus showing on its bones. Yes, the dinosaurs were terrible lizards. That's why they were given that name. You see, 'dino' means terrible, and 'saurus' means lizard. They are Greek words." Winkie lit a stubby pipe that he had pulled out of his pocket and puffed on it.

"Please tell us more about the dinosaurs," begged Chris.

"Yes, please do," added the boys. They were also eager to learn about the huge reptiles from Winkie.

The old man puffed a while on his pipe. After blowing out two or three long whiffs of smoke, he continued. "Well, bones have told the scientists that some of those strange-looking reptiles were as small as turkeys. Some were so big that no other land animal has ever compared with them in size."

"How did they find out about what they ate?" asked Chris.

"From the size and shape of the skeleton's teeth and its long sharp claws," answered Winkie. "The meat-eaters were two-footed and walked on their hind legs. They balanced themselves with their long, heavy tails, and they used their short front legs to tear apart the flesh of other dinosaurs. The plant-eaters were usually large, heavy, four-footed beasts. Many had long necks and tails." After a pause Winkie went on, "As you can see, there were many kinds of dinosaurs. That's why I'm so anxious to find the graveyard. A different species of dinosaur might be there that no one has ever seen before. Or there might be some fossilized eggs. It would be really something to come across those because no dinosaur eggs have been discovered in North America. A few fragments of shells in Montana are all that have been found. Whole eggs have been located in Asia, Europe, East Africa, and Brazil." Then the old man looked troubled, and the children were concerned.

"It's the map I'm thinking about," he explained. "I wonder why someone took it. Did the person know that my friend was a uranium prospector, and did that person believe he would find uranium? On the other hand no mention of uranium is made on the map. So whoever went off with it must be after the dinosaur graveyard."

"I'm sure it's the bald-headed man Chris and I saw last night," said Ken.

Winkie did not answer. "Let's see if there are any dinosaur bones left in this quarry."

He began searching among the broken pieces of sandstone. He ran his fingers along every one that looked promising, hoping to find a dinosaur bone sticking out.

The children did the same, but after a while they grew discouraged.

"We're wasting our time," said Ken. "There are no dinosaur bones here."

The old man smiled. "My, but you give up easily. Take a look at what I just found."

The children stared at a piece of skull protruding slightly from a layer of sandstone.

"It is such a small skull I think it might be from Diplodocus," said Winkie. "That dinosaur had a long neck, but a very small head."

"Yeah, that's right. From the pictures I've seen of Diplodocus in books its head was very small." Marty was as thrilled as if he had found the skull himself.

Chris was anxious to see how Winkie was going to dig it out of the rock. She watched with the boys as he chipped away very carefully at the sandstone with his chisel and pick.

Minutes went by. Winkie was still busy. Sweat rolled down his forehead, and his face was red from working in the hot sun.

"You know something?" he said, wiping his forehead with a big handkerchief. "I'm hungry. How about you?"

"I'm so hungry I could eat an elephant," answered Ken. "Or a dinosaur."

"So could I," added Marty.

"Okay. Let's have our lunch in the shade of that big boulder over there."

The children raced to the boulder, but they waited for Winkie before starting to eat the peanut butter sandwiches they had pulled out of their knapsacks.

"Boy, that tasted good," said Marty as he finished a sandwich.

Chris and Ken also agreed that they had never

eaten a better sandwich, but when Winkie opened a box of chocolate cookies that Mrs. Winkle had sent along, their mouths began to water all over again.

After the children had scooped out the last crumbs in the box, they went back to the quarry with Winkie. This time they dug out the rest of the skull under his guidance. Then, wanting to find a skull of their own, they began hunting in the quarry for one.

Finally Chris gave a loud cry of joy.

Everyone came running.

"Here's a dinosaur tooth. See it!" Chris was on her hands and knees peering at the tooth in the sandstone.

"Sure enough," cried Winkie, with a big smile. "It looks like the tooth of Tyrannosaurus. It was a bloodthirsty dinosaur. Its six-inch teeth were as sharp as sabers. Good work, Chris."

Chris grinned with happiness. While Winkie showed her how to dig around the dinosaur tooth, the boys continued hunting in the quarry like a pair of eager bloodhounds.

It was not long before they each found a small, round stone that looked as if it had been polished by a jeweler. The boys showed them to Winkie, anxious to find out what they were.

"They are gizzard stones," he replied. "For many years these round stones with a high polish have been showing up in sedimentary rocks. Some scientists believe that the stones were swallowed by dinosaurs to help them digest their food, just as chickens swallow gravel for the same purpose. A mass of these round stones was found in Asia in a dinosaur skeleton but so far none has been found in the dinosaur skeletons in North America."

"That's interesting," said Marty. "I'm going to look for more gizzard stones."

The twins joined him; but the searching expedition did not last long, because Winkie decided it was time to leave.

"Couldn't we stay a little longer?" pleaded Chris. "We haven't found the dinosaur graveyard, and we promised you we would. Now I'm sure if we went to the other side of this cliff, we'd find a clue there."

"You could be right, Chris, but it would take hours to walk around this cliff. We've got to get back to camp before dark. I'll admit, though, it is discouraging not to come across one clue today."

"It certainly is," agreed Marty. "We're no

closer to finding the dinosaur graveyard than when we started searching this morning, but we did find a skull and some gizzard stones."

"Maybe we'll have more luck tomorrow," said Winkie.

The children immediately perked up. In fact, they wished it was tomorrow right now so that they could go back to hunting for the graveyard.

CHAPTER FIVE

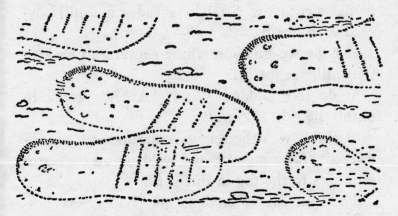

The Footprints

The next day Winkie drove his truck into dinosaur country again. The children were sitting in the front seat, gazing at the passing scenery.

"Those mountains look new to me," Chris remarked after quite a long drive.

"I thought we'd go to a different place to hunt for the dinosaur graveyard," said Winkie.

Chris was disappointed. She still felt there must be a clue on the other side of the cliff with the quarry. However, after Winkie parked his truck and they all got out, she began searching for a clue with the others.

They followed a path with some deer tracks

across a meadow. Straight ahead was a hill covered with brush.

"I hope we find something exciting in back of that hill," said Chris.

"I do too," added Marty. "Are we going to climb the hill, Winkie?"

"I think we'd better walk around it," he answered. "It's a big hill, and we'd get pretty warm climbing to the top in this sun."

The four hikers trudged on. It was very hot, and once Winkie asked them if they wanted to turn back. They did, but each one refused to admit it. So after what seemed a long time, they reached the other side of the hill. Then they stared round-eyed in amazement. About half a mile away was a camel-back cliff, and not far from it was a cliff with a big hole.

"Wow! We've found the two clues," shouted Marty, slapping his thighs with joy.

"Yippee! We're on the right track now," yelled Ken, turning a somersault.

Chris was so happy that she jumped up and down and raced around in a circle.

Winkie kept blinking hard to make sure he was seeing correctly. Then, after looking at the cliffs through his binoculars, he started walking rapidly toward them.

The children kept up with him. As soon as they reached the camel-back cliff, they ran their fingers very slowly over layers of sandstone along the bottom. When they did not find a trace of a dinosaur bone, they climbed part way up the cliff and continued hunting. Still they had no success, so Winkie suggested walking to the cliff with the big hole.

On the way the boys started to run ahead.

Winkie called to them. "You stay with me," he said sternly. "You can get lost in this rugged country."

Marty and Ken apologized for racing ahead and then stood still as Winkie began to yodel. He threw back his head and made his voice go up and down in trills.

The children were entranced. As they hiked on, they took turns trying to yodel. Their voices did not sound like Winkie's, but they enjoyed hearing their own echoes.

Finally Chris shouted at the top of her lungs. "We're almost there." She picked up a stone and threw it at the cliff with the big hole. It did not come anywhere near it.

The boys waited until they had walked a little further, and then they each threw a stone. Wham! Marty hit the side of the cliff. Ken missed, but he tried again. This time his stone struck the cliff. Delighted, he kept on throwing rocks until he heard Marty cry out, "Here are some footprints!"

The twins and Winkie came running. Getting down on their hands and knees, they looked at the footprints in the soft dirt.

"But they're the tracks of a person," cried Chris.

"Hm," said Winkie. "Fresh ones, too. They were made since the dew fell last night."

"And the person was wearing rubber-soled shoes," said Ken. "You can see the ridges across each footprint."

"You sure can!" Marty was looking at the tracks so closely that his nose almost touched them.

Chris had leaned back, but she was staring at the footprints with a sharp eye. Finally she gave her opinion of them. "The tracks show that the person was wearing large shoes. So he must have been a man."

"You've hit upon something, Chris," said Winkie, with a smile. He kept looking at the footprints while the children scattered to see what else they could find.

Soon Marty cried out again. "The man has been digging on the side of the cliff. You can see where he pulled out some rocks."

Winkie and the twins came quickly to the place where someone had removed several layers of sandstone.

"Boy, I'll bet he's hunting for the dinosaur graveyard," said Ken.

"I wouldn't be surprised," answered Winkie in a concerned voice. "Let's see if we can find some dinosaur bones."

For the next hour Winkie and the children searched along the side of the cliff, but all their efforts proved in vain.

"Shucks," groaned Marty. "We found the two clues. Now if we could figure out what the two blurred words mean in the map, we'd get somewhere."

"I agree with you," said Ken, "but those words have me stumped."

"Why don't we hunt around here some more?" suggested Chris. "Then maybe all of a sudden we'll find out what the two words mean."

"I wish we could stay longer," answered Winkie, "but we got started late this morning, so we should head back to camp now."

The children groaned with disappointment.

"I'll tell you what we'll do," said Winkie. "We'll leave at seven o'clock tomorrow morning. Then we can search most of the day for the dinosaur graveyard. Okay?"

"Fine," answered the boys.

Chris also was happy about Winkie's plans. The next morning at the appointed hour she and the boys went to Winkie's truck. He was already there, waiting for them.

As the truck chugged out of the camp grounds, Marty said to Winkie, "I have something very important to ask you."

"Go ahead. Shoot. I'm listening," replied the old man.

"Well, I read in a book that it was hard for Stegosaurus to escape from its enemies. So what did that dinosaur do when other dinosaurs attacked it?"

"That's a good question, Marty," replied Winkie. "Scientists have learned from studying a Stegosaurus skeleton that there were sharp spikes on its back and tail. They have also discovered that Allosaurus attacked Stegosaurus. Remember what I told you about that dinosaur the other day?"

"I do," Chris spoke up quickly. "Only I have a hard time keeping track of the names of those big dinosaurs."

"I'll write down their names for you," said Winkie. "I might even draw some pictures of the dinosaurs."

Chris's blue eyes sparkled with delight. "That would be wonderful, Winkie. When I go back to school in September, I'll show them to my class. You won't forget, will you?"

Winkie laughed. "No. You can count on me for a list of dinosaurs. Now to get back to Marty's question about Stegosaurus. It was hard for that armored dinosaur to run or wade into swamps to get away from its enemies. So when Allosaurus tried to attack Stegosaurus, it stood still and thrashed its tail, which was covered with big spikes. Those spikes were so strong that they crushed Allosaurus' ribs."

"Boy! That sure was something," said Marty. "Thanks for answering my question."

Then Marty looked at the countryside. "Aren't you taking a different road?" he asked Winkie.

"Yes, it's a short cut," answered the old man. He began to sing an old hillbilly song.

When he had finished, Chris pleaded with him

to sing it again. "I want to learn it," she said.

"Okay. Here I go," said Winkie. He had sung only the first line when BOOM BANG! filled the air. "A blowout!" he groaned, bringing the truck to a stop.

Everyone climbed out to look at the tire with the big hole in it.

"I helped Dad once when he had a flat tire," said Marty. "Where is your jack, Winkie?"

"Huh," snorted the old man as he looked in the rear of his truck. "I loaned my jack to a camper, and he forgot to put it back. Well, I should have checked before we left, but who in thunderation would have thought we'd have a blowout?"

"What do we do now, Winkie?" asked Chris with a worried expression on her freckled face.

Winkie put his arm around her. "The world hasn't come to an end. I'll walk to the main highway and get a lift to a gas station. You'll be all right here, won't you?"

"Sure," answered Marty. "We'll stand guard at the truck."

"Yes, you do that," replied the old man. "I won't be gone long."

CHAPTER SIX

The Wrong Turn

As soon as Winkie left for a jack to fix his flat tire, Chris and the boys sat down by the side of the road in the shade of the truck.

Minutes went by. They turned into half an hour, and the children began to grow restless. Marty got up and started to examine some rocks close by. As he turned one over, a queer-looking bug scooted this way and that way.

Just then Ken came to see what Marty was doing. After watching the bug a while, the boys rolled over a large rock to see if something was hiding underneath it. To their joy they found another unusual bug. While they were examining it,

Chris spotted a fairly large animal lying on the edge of a sagebrush flat across the road. It was a badger with silver-gray fur.

Chris rose slowly to her feet and started tiptoeing in that direction.

Suddenly the badger got up and hurried to its burrow close by. A second later it ducked into the hole.

Chris lost no time peering into the dark entrance. Then, scowling with disappointment because she could not see the badger, she decided to search elsewhere for another animal.

Presently she saw a jackrabbit sitting near some sagebrush. She smiled at the jackrabbit—a broad grin reaching from ear to ear. The rabbit did not budge an inch.

This encouraged Chris. She took one step, then another, toward the rabbit. Still it did not move. So Chris drew closer, and suddenly the rabbit went into action. It jumped away, then stopped and froze as rigid as a statue.

Chris continued to tiptoe nearer. Again the rabbit let her come close before it darted off.

This went on for quite a while, until finally the rabbit disappeared in some heavy brush.

Disgusted, Chris gave up the chase and looked

around for the pick-up truck. To her horror it was nowhere in sight.

Chris started to run. She thought she was going in the direction from which she had come but soon faced a grove of unfamiliar poplar trees.

"Ken, Marty," she yelled. "Where are you?"

There was a dead silence.

Chris ran farther, going by the tall poplars and a big boulder. Ahead of her lay a flat stretch of open land where juniper shrubs with sharp prickly leaves were growing. Chris stumbled into one of the shrubs but did not stop to see if she was hurt. Instead, she picked herself up in a hurry and raced on.

Finally Chris stopped running, and after getting her breath, called the boys again.

A squirrel chattered at her from a tree nearby. Chris did not even look at the animal. All she knew was that she was lost and that she must find her way back before the others went on without her. But they wouldn't do that, Chris reasoned. They would look for her.

Relieved by this thought, she sat down on a rock to rest.

All this while the boys had been turning over

more rocks and looking for bugs. Suddenly Ken noticed that his sister was nowhere around.

"Chris," he yelled.

There was no answer.

"Chris," shouted Marty.

Still there was silence.

Ken's heart began to pound. He knew that his sister liked to wander whenever they went anywhere. "I'll bet she's gone exploring, Marty," he wailed, "and she can't find her way back. We've got to find her."

Marty was as concerned as his friend. He looked to the left and right, wondering which way to go.

"We'd better start up the road," advised Ken in a worried voice.

Marty nodded, and together they set out at a rapid pace. They took turns calling Chris, but only the echoes of their voices came back to them.

At last, after walking half a mile, they heard an answer in the distance.

"That sounds like Chris," said Ken, running in the direction from which the cry had come.

Marty hurried, too. He and Ken dashed through brush and over rocks. They tore into some greasewood. Its prickly spines hurt the boys, but they kept on running.

By this time Chris had decided to stay where she was, on the rock, until she could see the boys. She continued calling to them, however, and they kept answering.

As Ken and Marty drew closer, Chris suddenly gave a loud scream.

The boys ran faster. They were certain that a big animal was attacking Chris.

In a few moments they saw her hurrying toward them. She was still screaming when she reached them.

"Are you all right?" asked Ken.

"Yes," muttered Chris between breaths. Then she said in an excited voice, "I saw a big snake. It puffed way up and hissed at me."

"Did it bite you?" asked Marty.

"No, but it was the biggest snake I've ever seen." Chris stretched her arms out to show how long it was. "I think it was a rattlesnake."

"If it swelled up and hissed, it was a bull snake," said Marty. "Winkie told me that a bull snake won't hurt you."

Chris looked disappointed. "Just the same it

scared me almost to death." Then she added, "Golly, I'm glad you found me. I don't know how I got lost. I was chasing a big rabbit, and before I knew it, I couldn't see Winkie's truck."

"We'd better start back right away," advised Marty. "Otherwise Winkie will think that all three of us are lost."

The boys began walking in the direction from which they had come. Chris did not have to hurry to keep up with them. They took their time, jumping over every rock they saw and at the same time getting off their course little by little.

Finally the boys came to a dead stop and looked around, trying to get their bearings.

"Which way do we go to get back to the road?" asked Ken.

"I don't know," answered Marty.

"Let's go to the left," suggested Ken.

Marty accepted his advice, but after he and the twins had walked a short distance, they came to a meadow. Indian paintbrush, a beautiful red flower, was growing near some yellow bee plant and daisies.

"We're all lost now," groaned Marty.

"We sure are," admitted Ken.

Chris began wiping tears out of her eyes. "It's all my fault," she sobbed. "If I hadn't chased that rabbit, we'd be by the truck waiting for Winkie. He's probably there by now."

"I guess he is," answered Ken. He wanted to tell her Winkie would never take them on a dinosaur hunt again, but Chris was crying so hard that he put one arm around her and said, "You didn't mean to get lost. Winkie will understand."

"Sure. Ken is right," added Marty. "Winkie is a swell guy. He won't be angry. I'll bet he's looking for us this very minute. Let's call him."

The children called as loudly as they could. They kept this up until Chris's voice gave out. All she could do was squeak, so she sat down on a flat rock in the sun. The boys joined her. Perspiration dripped from their foreheads and trickled down their cheeks, but no one complained of being hot. All they were concerned about was getting back to Winkie.

CHAPTER SEVEN

The Big Cat

After a brief rest, Marty and the twins trudged on, hoping they would reach Winkie. Instead, they were really going farther away from him and into country they had never seen before. They hiked around several hills and came to a valley with high bluffs on either side.

The twins hesitated, wondering if they should keep on.

"Let's go," urged Marty. "Here's a trail that could bring us out to a road, and we might find Winkie there."

Marty started hiking up the path, where a stream flowed rapidly over rocks. The twins followed. As they came to a big boulder that blocked most of the path, Marty cautiously walked around it. Chris drew back and stared at the stream. She knew that with one false step, she would fall into the water.

Ken sensed his sister's fear. "I'll help you," he said, holding out his hand.

Chris grabbed it and together they managed to get around the large rock. Then they trudged on, going around smaller boulders until at last they reached a turn near the end of the valley.

To their disappointment they found themselves at the entrance of a canyon. It was not as wide as the one they had walked through two days before, and the cliffs, instead of sloping, went straight up in the air.

"Let's see where this canyon comes out," suggested Marty.

"Okay," answered Ken, "but I think we're walking farther and farther away from camp."

"So do I," added Chris. "We've been hiking for miles and getting no place."

"Well, we can't just stand still," answered Marty. "We're bound to come to a road somewhere. So let's move on."

He led the way, and the twins followed close behind him.

Some swallows darted around the children, zooming low and then shooting upward like rockets. The boys watched the birds, fascinated by their flying pattern.

Chris was more interested in the sky, which looked like a long blue ribbon above the narrow canyon. When some black clouds appeared she became worried.

Shortly after that lightning zigzagged across the darkened heavens, and a loud rumble sounded in the distance.

"A thunderstorm is coming," yelled Chris. "I'm scared."

The boys were as frightened as she.

"We'd better get out of this canyon before the storm breaks," warned Marty. He started to run.

The twins kept up with Marty until Chris felt a sharp pebble in her shoe. While Ken was digging it out for her, several claps of thunder echoed in the canyon. Chris put her hands over her ears to soften the noise. Then her eyes opened wide with terror. Jagged streaks of lightning shot here and there along the cliffs. They looked very close.

"Come on," called Marty. He was waiting for his friends, and at the same time looking around frantically for shelter. He could see no hollow logs to crawl into, and he knew it was not safe to stand under a tree.

Chris and Ken caught up with Marty. They did not bother to explain why they were delayed, for the wind was blowing hard. It lashed the trees in front of them. As the children hurried past a pine, its low branches touched their heads. Big drops of rain were starting to fall, and one splashed on Chris's nose. She ran faster and almost bumped into Marty. He had spotted an overhanging cliff several yards away.

"Let's beat it over there," he shouted above the roar of the wind.

The children dashed for the shelter. They reached it just as a heavy curtain of rain poured down from the heavens.

Huddled together under the eaves of the overhanging cliff, Marty and the twins sat out the storm. Thunder crashed and boomed until the walls of the canyon seemed to be splitting apart. Never in all her life had Chris heard noise like this. Trembling from head to toe, she moved closer to her brother. Then, as lightning flashed everywhere in the canyon, Chris shut her eyes tight.

The boys were braver. They watched the lightning dance around them. They gasped, though, when it ripped the bark from the trunk of a tree only a stone's throw away.

"Boy, am I glad we didn't stand under that tree," said Ken.

Marty agreed and listened to the wind. It was not blowing as hard and the claps of thunder were not as loud.

Gradually the storm moved on, and the children breathed more easily.

"I don't know what would have happened to us if you hadn't seen this overhanging cliff," Ken told Marty.

"We would have been struck by lightning," said Chris. "You were smart to think of this place, Marty. It's like a little house, because it has a roof on it."

Marty's grin showed that he was pleased and proud.

When the rain stopped, the children continued walking in the canyon. They sloshed through deep water, getting more soaked by the minute. They did not mind, however, for the sun came out and dried their clothes. Then too, straight ahead the canyon widened out, and they hoped that Winkie might be waiting for them there in his truck.

Alas, this was not the case. When Chris and the boys came to the end of the canyon, there was no road in sight. All they saw was a valley and a river winding through it.

"Oh, dear. This is awful," cried Chris. "We'll never find Winkie."

"No, we won't," said Ken in despair.

Marty tried to stay calm. "Yes, we will," he assured them in a lighthearted voice. "If we follow the river, it will bring us back to camp."

The twins decided that was the only thing left to do. Soon they were all hiking along the river bank. It was not long, though, before the boys and Chris stopped and threw stones in the river. When they grew tired of doing this, they walked on in silence until Marty saw a fish pop out of the water.

"Man! Did you see that fish catch a bug?"

"Yeah," answered Ken. "I'll bet the river is loaded with fish. Boy, I could eat one right now."

"So could I," declared Marty. "Of course we would have to catch a fish first and then cook it. But I could start a fire without matches. I'll show you." He picked up two stones and rubbed them together. "A spark will come any minute," he said.

Chris and Ken watched closely, but nothing happened.

"Shucks," groaned Marty. "I've read about people doing this when they have no matches."

"Never mind, Marty," consoled Chris. "Even if you did start a fire, we have nothing to cook."

She and Ken walked on. Marty tried once more with the stones. He had no success, so he hurried to catch up with his friends.

After hiking a quarter of a mile or so, all three of them stopped cold in their tracks, staring in horror at a mountain lion, only a hundred feet away. The big cat appeared to be as surprised as they were.

"Don't move," whispered Marty.

Chris froze solid, and so did the boys. With pounding hearts they watched the mountain lion, who stared back with deep yellow eyes glistening in the sunlight. Not a muscle moved in its body. Even its long tail, which it held low, remained rigid.

Then suddenly the big cat turned and, taking giant leaps, headed for a sloping cliff.

The children took to their heels and ran as fast as they could away from the lion.

When they felt they were far enough away, they stopped to get their breaths.

"Whew! That was a close call," said Ken.

"It sure was," agreed Marty. "From what I've read about a mountain lion, it stays away from people unless it's hungry or wounded. Just the same, I feel you never can tell what an animal like that is going to do."

Chris swallowed hard. "Then it might come after us."

"You've got something there," said Ken. "Look at these big footprints."

"Wow!" cried Marty as he examined the fresh trail in the dirt. "I'll bet these belong to a mountain lion, and not the one we saw, either. They might be the female's footprints. We'd better follow the river upstream."

"That's where we just saw a mountain lion," said Ken.

"Yeah, I know," answered Marty, "but there are more footprints over there. See them?"

Chris was terrified. "There must be a whole lot of lions around here." She started to run up the river bank.

The boys raced after her.

CHAPTER EIGHT

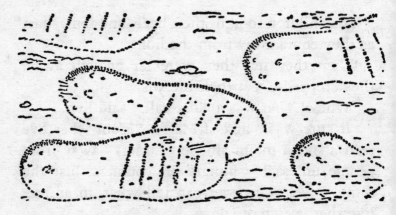

The Stranger

Chris ran past the place where they had seen the mountain lion. The boys, close at her heels, hurried just as quickly. Then, gasping for breath, they all stopped and stared up at the sloping cliff. All they could see were a few trees and some brush.

Still feeling uneasy, the children moved on, but they kept looking back to make sure the big cat was not on their trail. To their relief, only a squirrel was following them. In leaps and bounds the animal tagged after the three hikers until it finally ran up a tree and chattered at them.

After that all became quiet in the wilderness area—too quiet to suit the boys and Chris.

Suddenly they jumped in alarm and stared wide-eyed at some bushes where a mule deer was visible. As the animal bounded away, the children gave a relaxed sigh.

"I'm sure glad that wasn't the mountain lion," said Marty.

"So am I," answered Ken.

Chris did not say anything, but she stayed close to the boys as they continued walking along the river. The breeze fanning her face felt good in the hot sun, but she wished the wind would blow hard and really cool her off. Then she stopped short, and so did the boys. Only a few feet away an animal with quills on its back lay alongside a boulder.

"Don't go near that porcupine," warned Marty. "It thrashes its quills around whenever it's attacked. Why, I knew a dog that was killed by a porcupine's quills. They stuck in his nose and mouth, and he couldn't get them out."

Chris shuddered, but she took one more look at the porcupine before moving along with the boys.

It was not long before she felt Ken tugging at

her sleeve and pointing to another animal swimming in the river, with only its dark head above water.

"That's a muskrat," said Marty, who had also spotted the swimmer.

He hiked on with his friends, but they were all getting so tired that before long they walked at a slow pace.

Finally Chris felt she could not go a step farther. She sprawled out on the ground.

"Please keep moving," Marty begged her. "It's important that you do, Chris."

"I don't see why it is," she argued, slowly rising to her feet. "We'll never get back to camp, because we're following the river upstream and not downstream."

"But it's better than meeting several mountain lions," replied Marty. "Remember all those big footprints we saw? Besides, Winkie and a searching party will find us before long. You'll see that I'm right." His voice quivered, though, and Chris knew he was just trying to be brave.

For the next half hour she and the boys trudged along the river bank. Then Chris decided to rest on a log. This time Ken pleaded with her to go on, but she would not budge an inch.

"Everything has gone wrong," she wailed. "We were going to help Winkie find the dinosaur graveyard. Instead I got lost and made you get lost too. Now I'm so tired and hungry that I don't know what's going to happen to me."

The boys looked at her in concern. Then Ken put his arm around her, and she cried on his shoulder.

Marty stood there, wishing he could do something to comfort Chris, when suddenly something attracted his attention.

"Look!" he cried. "There's smoke ahead."

The twins stared at a thin stream of smoke curling lazily in the distance.

"Do you suppose Winkie started a fire, hoping we would see it?" asked Ken.

"I wouldn't be surprised," answered Marty. "Let's go and see." Marty was so excited that he fell over a rock in his haste, but he was up in a flash, hurrying with the twins toward the smoke.

As the children ran around a clump of trees, they came upon a tall, thin man broiling fish over a small fire. His pants and shirt were torn in several places, and his red cap had seen better days.

The man looked up and raised a bushy eyebrow in amazement when he saw the children. "What on earth are you doing here?" he asked them.

Marty immediately told the stranger how they had gotten lost.

"And we saw a mountain lion," finished Chris.

"A mountain lion, eh!" The man raised a bushy eyebrow again. "It's not often that you see one in this country. In fact, they are quite rare." After a pause he added, "If you had stayed put when you discovered you were lost, your friend Winkie would have found you. But don't feel badly. I've known grown people to do what you did. You've come a long way in one day. I'll cook you some dinner."

Chris clapped her hands. "That would be wonderful! I was afraid we'd starve to death." Then in a concerned voice she said, "I wish you had a telephone so that I could let Mother know where we are. She worries something awful when my brother and I are late for dinner."

"I'm sure the searchers are out looking for you," answered the stranger, "but I don't think they'll find you before morning."

"I was hoping they would real soon," said Marty.

"My mom worries too if I'm not home by six

o'clock." He shook his head. "Boy, this is terrible."

"It sure is," agreed Ken, biting his lip nervously.

"Well, one thing should console you," said the stranger. "You won't have to sleep out in the open tonight. I'll put you up in my cave, and in the morning I'll see that you get back to your parents."

"Swell," said Marty. "We'd appreciate it very much."

"We certainly would," added the twins and then watched the stranger walk to a large, dark opening in the side of a cliff close by.

As he crawled inside, Ken said to his sister, "He looks like the man we saw at camp the night Winkie's map was stolen."

Chris hesitated. "I'm not sure. We can't tell if this man is bald because he's wearing a cap."

"I'll bet he *is* bald," answered Ken.

Marty was trying to remember where he had seen the stranger before. Was it back home? Or was it somewhere else, he asked himself.

Just then Marty's thoughts were interrupted as he heard Ken exclaim, "Take a look at his footprints! They're exactly like the ones we saw at the camel-back cliff."

Marty and Chris began examining the tracks. They could see the ridges from a rubber-soled shoe going across each footprint.

"Am I right?" asked Ken.

"Yes," admitted Chris.

Marty nodded. "Let's see what he's doing in the cave."

He started walking toward it. Chris and Ken followed. They found the stranger circling a flashlight around the inside of the cave. The air was cool, and the walls and ceiling were as dry as a parched leaf.

"I'm hunting for some root bulbs that I stored in here," he explained to the children.

Marty and the twins did not appear interested, for something had caught their attention—a dead rabbit hanging from a peg on the wall. Alongside the rabbit stood a rifle.

The man noticed how frightened the children looked, especially Chris. Her face had turned white.

"Don't let the dead rabbit scare you," he said. "I shot it this morning. You see, I'm trying to live off the land the way the Indians did. Of course they hunted with bow and arrow, and I used a gun. Maybe you'd rather have fish for dinner instead of rabbit?"

"Yes, please," answered Chris quickly. "I couldn't bear to eat a rabbit. That's how I got lost—chasing a rabbit because I wanted to pet it."

"Then, little princess, you shall have fish. Ah, here are the sego lily bulbs." The man picked up a handful of them. "They really taste good once they're roasted."

The children did not say anything. They followed the stranger back to his fire and helped him put on more kindling wood.

When the food was ready, Chris washed her hands in the river and urged Ken to do the same.

"Shucks! I want to eat," he answered.

"Me, too," chimed in Marty.

Chris shrugged. "I just don't like to eat with dirty hands."

She sat down on the ground with the boys and ate every bit of food that the man had placed on a tin plate for her.

"That was the best meal I've ever had," said Chris. "Thank you, Mr. . . . er . . . ?"

"Mr. Carpenter," finished the man.

Chris cocked her head in surprise. "I've never heard that name before. Are you a carpenter?"

The man laughed. "No. I'm a geologist. I'm prospecting for oil in this country. I'm surprised you didn't see my tools in the cave."

"I did," Ken spoke up quickly. "They're the same kind of tools that we use for dinosaur hunting. Are you looking for dinosaur bones, Mr. Carpenter?"

"No. Why do you ask?"

"Oh, I thought that maybe you were, since this is dinosaur country."

"Indeed it is," said Mr. Carpenter. "Most of the cliffs around here are made of sandstone, and that's where you are likely to come across a dinosaur skeleton. No, I'm not a dinosaur hunter, but I did find a fossil yesterday." He reached into his pocket and pulled it out for the children to see.

"Why, it looks like a leaf buried in a stone," said Chris.

"That's what a fossil is, little princess," replied Mr. Carpenter. "It's the remains of a prehistoric animal or plant that has become preserved in rock. This fossil is a gingko leaf from a tree that grew in this country about one hundred and thirty-five million years ago, when it was steaming swampland. These mountains, which are part of the Rocky Mountain system, did not exist then."

"How did the mountains get here?" asked Chris.

"That's a good question, and I'll try my best to answer it. Some scientists think that our planet is about five billion years old. In the beginning, there was no land as we know it, only water and bare rocks. The first animals were one-celled, tiny creatures that lived in the sea. Later, reptiles appeared on the earth, and some of the early ones were dinosaurs. At the end of the Age of Reptiles, the swamps began to shrink, and forests grew where there had been palms and ferns. Then a long time after that, some powerful forces inside the earth made the outer crust buckle. It wrinkled into long folds, and a broad strip of land bulged up many thousand feet above sea level and became the Rocky Mountains. Of course this did not happen overnight. Goodness, no! It took millions of years, and during that time the land sank and lifted more than once. Then decay and erosion set in. That's how these cliffs were formed. You know what erosion is, don't you?"

Chris frowned. She was not sure, and so she was glad when Marty quickly replied, "It's when water and wind beat against the land and wear it down. Glaciers and landslides will also do that."

"You're right," said Mr. Carpenter. "Years of erosion have made these cliffs and mountains as they are today."

"Thank you, Mr. Carpenter, for answering my question," said Chris.

"You're welcome. I think you and the boys had better turn in. You have had a long day, and you must be tired."

"Oh, but I'm not, Mr. Carpenter," cried Chris. "I'd love to find a fossil like yours."

"So would I," added Marty.

Ken was just as enthusiastic, but Mr. Carpenter was firm. "You can hunt for fossils tomorrow. Now let's head for my cave. It isn't big enough to hold four of us, so I'll use my sleeping bag and park under the tree outside."

A short while later the children were sprawled out in the cave on a bed of pine boughs that Mr. Carpenter had laid on the floor for them.

"Hey, Marty," Ken said in a low voice. "Are you awake?"

"Yes. Why?"

"I've been thinking about Mr. Carpenter. I'm sure he took Winkie's map and that he's after the dinosaur graveyard."

Chris had almost dozed off, but her brother's remark made her wide awake. "Ken, how can you talk that way about Mr. Carpenter after he's been so nice to us?"

"Yeah, I know," replied Ken. "He gave us something to eat and turned his cave over to us. Just the same, there are some things I can't figure out about Mr. Carpenter. He said he wasn't hunting for dinosaur bones, and yet he has dinosaur tools. Then there are his footprints. You both agreed with me that they looked like the ones we saw at the camel-back cliff."

"But you have no proof that Mr. Carpenter took Winkie's map," argued Chris.

"Your sister is right," said Marty.

Ken grumbled to himself. A few moments later he said, "Hey, Marty. I just thought of something else about Mr. Carpenter."

There was no answer from Marty. He was dead to the world, and so was Chris.

Ken lay awake a little longer. Then he too fell into a sound sleep.

CHAPTER NINE

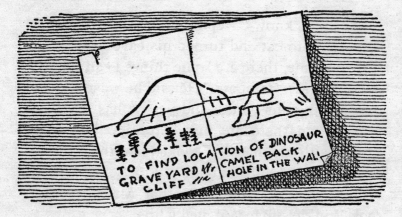

The Old Newspaper

When the children awoke the next morning, they sat up with a start—first Ken, then Marty, and last Chris. They blinked hard, wondering where they were in the darkness. Suddenly it dawned on them that they had spent the night in a cave.

"Man!" exclaimed Marty, his voice filled with excitement. "I can hardly wait to tell our friends back home about this experience. It is something very special to sleep in a cave."

"Yes, it is," agreed Chris. "I'll never forget it as long as I live."

Ken added his praise and then said, "Where do you suppose Mr. Carpenter is?"

Ken crawled out of the cave, and Marty and Chris followed. They were delighted to see the man placing food on a makeshift table.

"You're just in time for breakfast," he said. "I hope you don't mind fish and sego lily bulbs again."

The boys gulped, so Chris decided she had better say something. "Oh, that's all right, Mr. Carpenter. We love fish."

She sat down at the rickety table and began eating with the boys.

After they had finished, Mr. Carpenter walked with them down the river bank and beside the stream for about an hour.

"We should meet some of the searching party soon," he said as they hiked along.

Marty and the twins kept looking for the searchers. Finally they saw three men in the distance. They called loudly to them.

It was Winkie, Mr. Rockhill, and Mr. Taylor. They heard the children's shrill voices and walked quickly toward them.

Marty and the twins hurried too.

Before long Chris and Ken fell into the arms of their dad, and all three of them began kissing each other—they were so happy.

After that the children turned to Winkie.

"Am I glad we found you," he said, putting his arms around them. "I'll never forgive myself, though, for going off and leaving you alone."

"It was all my fault," said Chris. "I was chasing a big rabbit and got lost. Then the boys came and found me, but they got lost too—on account of me."

Ken spoke up to defend his sister. "Chris didn't get lost on purpose, Winkie."

"I'm sure she didn't," replied the old man.

Chris grabbed her brother's hand and gave it a grateful squeeze.

By this time Mr. Carpenter had joined the group. Marty introduced him, and Chris told how good he had been to them.

"It was mighty nice of you, Mr. Carpenter, to take care of the children," said Mr. Rockhill.

"I found it a pleasure to have three unexpected guests walk in on me," he answered. "Well, I guess I'd better get back to my oil prospecting. I'll stop by and see you one of these days."

"That would be wonderful, Mr. Carpenter," said Chris. "I'll look forward to it."

"Okay, little princess." With that the man went his way, and the others, after saying good-by, walked to Winkie's pick-up truck. Then the men got into the front seat, and the children climbed into the back. They rode quite a distance before they reached the turn into the camp grounds.

The first one to see the children was Mrs. Rockhill. She shouted to the other campers of their arrival, and everyone came running. The twins gave their mother extra long hugs.

Mrs. Rockhill smiled happily. "My prayer was answered. I had visions of wild animals attacking you, but you're not hurt one bit. You must be hungry, though, so I'll get Marty and you something to eat right away."

"Hey, Marty," said Ken. "How about having a second breakfast with Chris and me?"

"Sure," answered Marty, suddenly realizing he was hungry. He turned to his mother, who was wiping tears from her eyes. "Don't cry any more, Mom."

"I know it's silly of me," she replied, "but it's just that I am so glad you're alive. Tell the twins I have plenty of food ready. They can eat with you."

After Marty delivered his mother's message, he broke into a run for his camp site.

The twins raced after him. Then, breathless, they followed Marty into his tent.

"I want to look up something," he explained, feeling around the inside of his sleeping bag. "Yep, here it is." He pulled out a newspaper and stared at a photograph on the front page. "I knew I'd seen Mr. Carpenter's face before. See! Here's his picture."

The twins looked in astonishment at the photo of Mr. Carpenter.

"I found the newspaper in the trash can when I was looking for Winkie's map," continued Marty. "I was saving it to read about the kids who discovered some fossilized bones of a prehistoric camel. Now it's more important to read about Mr. Carpenter."

Marty and the twins began reading the account, which told that Mr. Carpenter was a geologist who was prospecting for oil in Utah. The write-up also mentioned that he had discovered some dinosaur bones in Wyoming.

"I was right, Ken!" exclaimed Chris. "Mr. Carpenter didn't take Winkie's map, because he isn't the man we saw that night around here. You can tell from this picture that he's not bald. He's got dark, wavy hair. So he isn't after the dinosaur graveyard."

"I wouldn't be too sure if I were you," warned Ken. "We saw Mr. Carpenter's footprints at the camel-back cliff. So what was he doing there?"

"Prospecting for oil," answered Chris quickly.

"Well, it seems mighty strange that of all the cliffs in this country, he should select that particular one," argued Ken. "Besides, it says in the newspaper that he found some dinosaur bones in Wyoming. So he must be a dinosaur hunter."

Chris frowned. She decided she would have to give that some thought before answering her brother.

Marty had not been listening to their conversation, for his thoughts were elsewhere.

"Boy, I wish we could go to the cliff with the big hole," he said.

Ken grinned. "I'm glad *you* feel that Mr. Carpenter is after the dinosaur graveyard."

"I don't," answered Marty. "I want to go there to prove something."

Ken was curious. "You sound mysterious. What do you want to prove?"

"It's the two blurred words in the map. I think I know what they mean."

"Golly, you do?" Chris was all ears. "Tell us, Marty."

Marty shook his head. "No, not now. Let's

have a second breakfast before we ask Winkie to take us dinosaur hunting."

The twins thought Marty's suggestion was a good one. After they had finished eating, they thanked Mrs. Taylor, and then hurried with Marty to Winkie's camp site.

The old man was sitting at the picnic table, studying his map. Beside it was the dinosaur list that he was making for Chris.

"Oh, Winkie, you found the map!" cried Chris.

"Mrs. Winkle picked it up in some brush on the other side of camp," he replied. With a sheepish expression he added, "I must have forgotten to close my fossil book when I laid my map on it, and the wind blew it away."

"Well, anyway, I'm glad you have the map," said Chris. "Now we can go and hunt for the dinosaur graveyard."

"Good heavens!" exclaimed the old man. "I should think you'd be dead tired after all the tramping you did yesterday."

"We're not," Marty assured him. "We had a good night's sleep in Mr. Carpenter's cave, and I've been thinking a lot about the blurred words in the map, Winkie. I want to see if I'm right about them. So could we please go to the cliff with the big hole?"

Winkie immediately became interested. He looked at his wrist watch. "It's almost eleven o'clock. We'll have to leave right away. That is, if you can get your parents' permission."

"We will," cried three children at once.

CHAPTER TEN

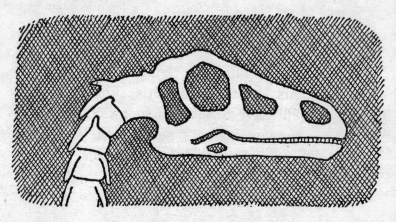

The Needed Words

Chris and the boys were unable to get their parents' permission to go dinosaur hunting again. So they asked Winkie to intercede for them. He agreed, and after talking with Mr. Rockhill and Mr. Taylor, he managed to get their consent.

Soon after that, Winkie left with the three youngsters in his pick-up truck for another dinosaur trip. He drove several miles before he parked his truck. Then he and the children started hiking to their destination. They walked across the large meadow and around the big hill. From there they headed in the direction of the cliff with the hole. As they drew near it, they saw a man digging there.

"It's Mr. Carpenter!" cried Ken.

"It must be somebody else," said Chris.

She and the boys wanted to run, but they kept on walking with Winkie.

Finally they came close enough to get a good look at the man's face.

"It *is* Mr. Carpenter!" exclaimed Ken. "He's after the dinosaur graveyard."

"Now, Ken, it's wrong to accuse someone unless you're sure," admonished Winkie.

Just then Mr. Carpenter waved, and the old man and the children hurried toward him.

When they reached Mr. Carpenter, Chris grabbed his hand. "I'm glad to see you so soon," she told him.

"So am I, little princess," he answered.

"We're going to hunt for the dinosaur graveyard," Chris went on merrily. "Only we're not sure whether it's at the camel-back cliff or this one."

"I didn't know there was a dinosaur graveyard around here," said Mr. Carpenter.

"You mean you're not looking for it?" asked Ken in surprise.

"Goodness, no! I was prospecting for oil at the camel-back cliff the other day. So I thought I'd hunt here today."

Ken hung his head. "I was sure you were after the dinosaur graveyard, and I'm sorry, Mr. Carpenter. You see, we saw your footprints at the camel-back cliff, and I . . ." Ken could not finish. He felt all choked up.

"That's all right," said Mr. Carpenter. "I don't wonder that you were suspicious when you saw my footprints. I guess my tools threw you off, too."

Ken nodded. "Yes, they did."

"Well, Ken, everyone who works with rocks uses about the same tools. I find a chisel, rock hammer, and prospector's pick mighty handy when I'm looking for specimens of rocks that might indicate oil formations."

"I'm glad you told me that," murmured Ken.

"So think nothing more about it, my boy. I forgive you."

Ken looked up with a relieved smile. "Will you help us hunt for the dinosaur graveyard?"

"Yes, if you really want me to."

"We certainly do," answered Winkie. "Maybe you'd like to see my map before we start searching for dinosaur bones?"

"Yes I would," replied Mr. Carpenter. He studied the map carefully. "Hm. Those two blurred words make it difficult to find the exact location of the graveyard."

"I think I know what the words mean," Marty spoke up quickly. "Could we climb to the ledge near the big hole, Winkie? We've hunted at the camel-back cliff and around here, but we haven't looked on that ledge."

"All right," said Winkie. "Let's go there."

Soon Winkie, Mr. Carpenter, and the children were climbing up the side of the sloping cliff to the wide ledge. When they reached it, Marty cried out, "Look! You can see the camel-back cliff through the hole in the wall."

"Well, I declare! So you can." Winkie was amazed.

The others were too. Then Chris repeated what Marty had just said, " 'You can see the camel-back cliff through the hole in the wall.' I get it! The two blurred words in the map are *see* and *through*."

"That's right!" exclaimed Ken. Then he repeated what was written on the map, and put in the blurred words. " 'To find the location of the dinosaur graveyard *see* the camel-back cliff

through hole in the wall.' Why, the graveyard is here on the ledge. Man! Are you smart to figure that out, Marty."

"Golly, I'll say you are!" Chris looked at Marty in admiration.

"Oh, it wasn't too hard," he replied.

"It took a lot of thinking on your part," said Winkie, "and I'm proud of you."

Marty grinned from ear to ear.

It was not long before they all began hunting for the dinosaur graveyard on the ledge. However, the more they searched for it, the more they wondered if the graveyard *was* there.

Finally the twins began poking around some brush where the ledge met the wall of the cliff.

"Here's the dinosaur graveyard or at least part of it!" they shouted.

Winkie and the others came running.

"It certainly is!" exclaimed the old man, staring at part of a dinosaur tail sticking out of a layer of sandstone.

Marty was just as thrilled. "Wow! You've got sharp eyes to find this," he said to the twins.

"You helped too," replied Chris. "We wouldn't have looked on this ledge if you hadn't figured out the two blurred words."

"You're right," said Winkie. "All three of you had a part in discovering the dinosaur graveyard, and I don't know how to thank you."

"You don't have to thank us, Winkie," said Chris, "because we haven't found out what the dinosaur skeleton looks like."

"Indeed, we haven't," added Mr. Carpenter. "Let's all of us start digging and see what we uncover."

The children thought that was a good idea. They cleared away some of the brush with the men. Then they used their tools to uncover more of the tail.

In an hour's time their efforts brought results. The entire tail, which was four feet long, lay exposed in the sandstone.

"Yippee! We're making progress," said Marty. "We sure are," added the twins.

The men laughed at the children's enthusiasm, but they were just as excited. They worked with them, and before too long, they managed to uncover the limbs of the skeleton. Next came the ribs, and finally the neck and skull.

As everyone stared in awe at the eight-foot skeleton, Marty asked Winkie what kind it was.

"I don't know," replied the old man.

"Neither do I," said Mr. Carpenter, "but I have a friend who can tell us. He's a paleontologist and lives about fifty miles from here. I'll give you his telephone number, Winkie, and you can call him tonight. I'm sure he'll be glad to look at this skeleton."

That evening Winkie phoned the paleontologist and told him about the dinosaur graveyard. The man was so interested that he arrived early the next morning to go with Winkie and the children. Mr. Carpenter was already at the foot of the cliff, prospecting for oil and at the same time watching that no other dinosaur hunter discovered the skeleton.

As soon as the paleontologist had examined the remains of the dinosaur, he said in an excited voice, "You've found a Camptosaurus, and it's very rare that you come across a perfect skeleton like this one. Why, the limbs are in their right positions, and the skull isn't broken. You've made a real contribution to science."

Winkie was so overcome with joy that he was speechless. The children were so thrilled that they could not stop talking about the Camptosaurus skeleton.

"I wish a lot of people could see it," said Chris.

"They can if Winkie will give the skeleton to a museum," answered Marty.

"It's your skeleton as much as mine," said Winkie, "and I think it's a wonderful idea to have the remains of a Camptosaurus dinosaur mounted in a big city museum."

Chris clapped her hands with delight. "Golly, hundreds of people are going to see our Camptosaurus skeleton. Now all we have to do is keep digging in this graveyard until we uncover the remains of another dinosaur."

"Or some dinosaur eggs," added Ken.

"Boy, that would be something," said Marty. "We would be the first to discover dinosaur eggs in North America. Let's get to work right now!"

Chris and Ken's List of Dinosaurs

ALLOSAURUS (Al-lo-sawr-us)

Description: The mighty hunter and a meat-eater. It had enormous jaws, many teeth, a large body, and a long tail. Allosaurus walked only on its hind legs, using its tail for balancing. Some Allosaurus dinosaurs were thirty-five feet long.

Habits: It used the hooklike claws on the ends of its short forelegs and its long jaws and bladelike teeth to tear the flesh off the bones of other dinosaurs.

ANKYLOSAURUS (An-kyle-o-sawr-us)

Description: An armored dinosaur and a plant-eater. It had short legs, a wide flat body protected by spikes and bony plates, and a stiff tail with a knob at the end. Some Ankylosaurus dinosaurs were fifteen feet long.

Habits: It used its tail when attacked, by thrashing it back and forth, thus giving crushing blows to its enemies, especially flesh-eating dinosaurs.

BRACHIOSAURUS (Brak-e-o-sawr-us)

Description: The heaviest of all dinosaurs and a plant-eater. It had a big body, long tail, long thick neck, and nostrils on top of its head. Its front legs were heavier and longer than its back legs. Some Brachiosaurus dinosaurs weighed fifty tons.

Habits: It was so heavy that it liked to stand in swamps where water helped to hold it up. Brachiosaurus also used swamps for protection, since it was slow-moving on land.

BRONTOSAURUS (Bron-to-sawr-us)

Description: The thunder lizard and a plant-eater. It had a long neck and tail and a huge body. Its head was very small, and its teeth were weak. Some Brontosaurus dinosaurs were seventy feet long and weighed thirty tons.

Habits: It spent a good deal of time in swamps and in the shallows of lakes and rivers where the water acted as a support. Brontosaurus also used swamps to escape from enemies that could not follow it into the water.

CAMPTOSAURUS (Camp-to-sawr-us)

Description: A duck-billed dinosaur and a plant-eater. It had powerful hind legs and a full set of fingers on each of its short forelegs. Camptosaurus walked on its hind legs but could easily get down on its four legs when feeding. Some Camptosaurus dinosaurs were fifteen feet long.

Habits: It lived on the ground and on the edges of swamps and marshes. Being very agile, Camptosaurus was able to escape from its enemies.

DIPLODOCUS (Di-plod-o-kus)

Description: The longest of all the dinosaurs and a plant-eater. It had an extremely long neck and tail and a long, thick body. Its head and mouth were very small, and its teeth were weak. Some Diplodocus were eighty feet long.

Habits: It spent most of its time eating plants, as Brontosaurus and Brachiosaurus did.

IGUANODON (I-gwan-o-don)

Description: A duck-billed dinosaur and plant-eater. It had a horny-beaked bill, a thick heavy tail and body, and a spike on its thumb. Iguanodon could walk on either two or four feet. Some Iguanodon dinosaurs were thirty feet long.

Habits: It lived in marshy or wet places and could stay under water to escape from its meat-eating enemies.

ORNITHOLESTES (Orn-i-tho-les-teez)

Description: A bird-stealer and meat-eater. It had a slim body, long legs, and a very long tail. Ornitholestes ran swiftly on its two-pronged hind feet. Some Ornitholestes dinosaurs were six feet long.

Habits: It used the long, clawlike fingers on its short forelegs to snatch birds from nests and perches and to catch lizards and other small ground-living animals.

OVIRAPTOR (Ovi-rapt-or)

Description: A very small dinosaur and egg-eater. It had a thin body, long neck and tail, and a small head. Oviraptor had short forelegs and walked only on its long hind legs. Some Oviraptor dinosaurs were three feet long.

Habits: It had no teeth and obtained its food by digging up and sucking the eggs of other dinosaurs.

PLESIOSAUR (Plees-i-o-sawr)

Description: A marine dinosaur and meat-eater. Some had long necks, long tails, and small heads. Others had short necks and long heads. Their broad, flat bodies had powerful flippers, which enabled them to swim backward and forward. Some Plesiosaur dinosaurs were fifteen feet long, others as long as forty feet.

Habits: It shot out its neck when catching a fish and held the fish fast in its mouth with its sharp teeth.

PROTOCERATOPS (Prot-o-ser-at-ops)

Description: One of the first horned dinosaurs and a plant-eater. It had a parrot beak and a wide shield of bones that covered the back of its neck. Protoceratops walked on its short forelegs and long hind legs. Some Protoceratops dinosaurs were eight feet long.
Habits: It laid its eggs in sandy hollows. Some of its eight-inch fossilized eggs have been found in the Gobi Desert.

STEGOSAURUS (Steg-o-sawr-us)

Description: An armored dinosaur and plant-eater. It had a small head, four stout legs, and large armored plates down the middle of its back. Its tail was equipped with four huge spikes. Some Stegosaurus dinosaurs were twenty feet long.
Habits: It lived on land and protected itself by swinging its tail from side to side and crushing the ribs of meat-eating dinosaurs.

TRICERATOPS (Try-ser-a-tops)

Description: An armored dinosaur and plant-eater. It had a huge squat body, short thick legs, and a short tail. Its head was enormous and ended in a shield. Above its parrot beak, a horn stuck out on its nose. Two other long horns stood out above its eyes. Some Triceratops dinosaurs were thirty feet long.
Habits: It lived on land and was a terrible fighter. Every other dinosaur, except Tyrannosaurus, was afraid of it.

TYRANNOSAURUS (Tye-ran-o-sawr-us)

Description: The tyrant lizard and meat-eater. Sometimes Rex or King is added to its name because it is believed to have been the most destructive of all dinosaurs. It had an enormous body, a long thick tail, and a huge head with a mouth filled with six-inch daggerlike teeth. Tyrannosaurus had short clawed forelegs and walked on its clawed hind feet, using its long thick tail as a balancer. Some Tyrannosaurus dinosaurs were fifty feet long and weighed about ten tons.
Habits: It preyed on other dinosaurs, attacking them with its claws and clamping down on their flesh with its powerful jaws and sharp teeth.

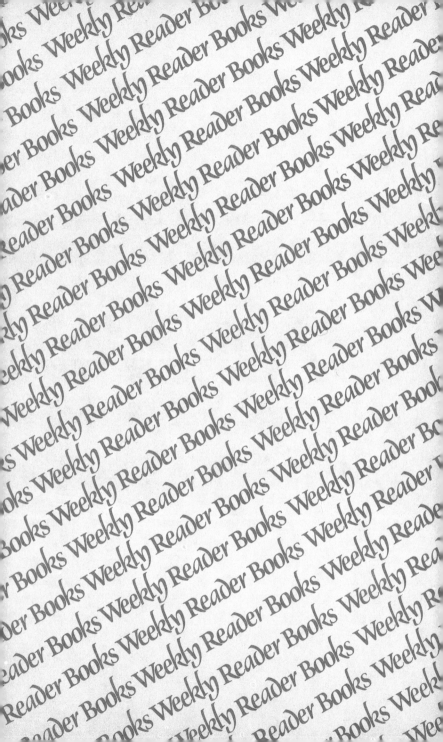